CH00802354

DRAGONS IN
DISGUISE

I. R. Davies

DaviesDuo

To Isaac and Oskar
Always believe in magic!
I. R. Davies
08. 05. 2021

Cover design by: I. R. Davies and T. L. Davies
Cover illustration designed by: dgim-studio / Freepik
Edited by: T. L. Davies
Printed in the United Kingdom

'I. R. Davies is a real talent for the future! A wonderful story that children will love. Beautifully written.'

Colin A. Millar, author of *'Leila's Game'* and *'Movie World'*

To Mammy, for helping me make my dream come true, and to Clover, for keeping me entertained when I was working on the less exciting parts of making a book!

To all young people reading this: a ten year old writing a book proves dreams can come true if you work hard enough!

Contents

✳ ✳ ✳

1. The Last Dragons?

It was a peaceful day on Earth, as all the dragons were carrying out their daily hunting. HydraHunters; purple and blue dragons, who swam in rivers, canals, lakes, and, more commonly, in the sea, were on the hunt for fish in the murky water below. The MoodDrifters; multi-coloured dragons, that changed colour depending on how they felt, were searching in the rainforests for tasty moss. FlameFlyers; dragons with fiery scales that scorched anything they touched, were hunting near the volcanos for appetising animals to eat.

Then there were the size-changing dragons, SilentSoarers; similar in appearance to butterflies, who were looking for giant flowers full of pollen. LeafCrawlers, who could camouflage themselves in their natural environment, were munching happily on bugs, whilst the RogueRacers; who resembled wasps in appearance *and* personality, were searching for other dragons to annoy! The nocturnal TwilightTwirlers, however, were asleep in their enormous caves.

It was beautiful at night. The TwilightTwirlers would search for their dinner (usually pouncing on animals while they were sleeping), and there would be a watery, shimmering light surrounding the dragons' lairs. You are probably wondering how that light was produced as electricity was not invented then. Maybe, it was the moon? No, it was the HydraHunters; their scales glowing brightly in the dark. The radiant light could be seen for miles.

But then it all went wrong; The light from the TwilightTwirlers attracted a DragonReaper; a dragon believed to be extinct. The DragonReaper slaughtered all the dragons while they slept, after first destroying the TwilightTwirlers. Eventually the DragonReaper died of old age – was its actions the cause of dragon extinction?

Nearly.

Millions of years later, when humanity eventually joined the planet, they were unaware that there were seven dragons still on Earth. Seven dragons, one of each species, and all in disguise...

2. Neigh-Neigh And Moo

Neigh-Neigh and Moo were sister and brother, who lived on a farm. These were not their real names, of course. Sarah Shell earned her family nickname from her love of horses, while Ben's job was to look after the cows, which he thoroughly enjoyed. Unfortunately, in school, children would make animal noises at Ben and Sarah, and shout, 'Oi, what's that smell? It's Neigh-Neigh and Moo! Stay away!'. Ben hated anyone who made fun of his sister and he got into trouble *every* day for it. He even punched Hugh in the nose when he galloped down the corridor and neighed at Sarah. Sarah never really minded the insults though, she always tried to look on the bright side; at least the children didn't say she looked like a horse!

Their teacher was called Mrs. Hound, and Sarah adored her. She was a tall lady, with a sharp nose that held red, square glasses. She always wore her brown hair in a tight plait. The teacher had a nice smile, when she used it, and always wore a black skirt, tights, and patterned long-sleeved tops. Mrs. Hound had a soft spot for Sarah because she handled her classmates' unkindness in such a positive way.

Sarah was nearly eleven and Ben would be ten in less than twenty-four hours! The family had a Border Collie called Dog who loved to spend time with the sheep, protecting them from animals that lived in the nearby woods. Dog would growl just thinking of these animals hurting his sheep! The Shell family also owned a cat called Mittens, who made sure that all mice and spiders in the tractor shed would be regularly killed and eaten. Overall, the Shell family were a very happy family. Even when one of their lambs would get caught and eaten by a wild animal, they would still try to find something good in the everyday. Even when the youngest members of the family were nicknamed 'Neigh-Neigh' and 'Moo'!

Sarah and Ben's dad was called Andy, and he was amazing with the farm animals, especially the chickens. Mr. Shell had a world record for being able to encourage a chicken into laying fifteen eggs in sixty seconds! Rita, his wife, cooked, cooked and... can you guess? You got it! Cooked! Mrs. Shell did not hold a world record but making a fifteen-egg omelette certainly deserved a medal!

The farm had a stable that was home to four horses; a large brown horse called Toffee who Mr. Shell would ride, a medium-sized black and white horse named Stormy for Mrs. Shell, a small jet-black horse called Shadow who belonged to Ben, and a tall white horse with black speckles around her legs called Snowball. She was Sarah's pride and joy. Snowball and Sarah were a wonderful team. Sarah had a huge shelf full of showjumping trophies earned by working with Snowball. She had another competition next Tuesday and was really looking forward to it.

One day, Sarah went into the corn field to get some food for her beloved horse, when she heard movement and strange sounds in the woods. She cautiously walked over. *It's probably just a fox tangled up in the brambles* she thought, bravely. She walked slowly towards the sound, left foot then right foot. The shuffling noises grew louder, and Sarah was sure she could hear growling. Suddenly, from out of the trees jumped an enormous black beast, dragging Sarah up into the sky with its giant feet; its wings beating wildly in the wind. Sarah screamed for her life, in hope that her father; her mother; Ben; even Dog or Mittens would hear her and help save her from the monster! But nobody heard her screams.

The creature carried her away, high up into the sky, through the clouds, far away from her family and her home. After what seemed like hours, it glided downwards onto an unexplored island, and laid her softly on the sand.

* * *

3. Ben's Birthday

Later that morning, Ben was washing the dishes when his mother came into the kitchen and asked, "Ben, is Neigh-Neigh up yet?" Ben shrugged his shoulders. "No, but it *is* half-term mum, so she is probably still in bed. Oh, mum-" he shouted to his mother as she was about to go upstairs. "One more day until my birthy birthy *birthday!*" His mother smiled back at him, her chocolate-brown eyes glistening. "Yes Moo, I know! Right, let me check on your sister." With that, she sprinted up the stairs.

Ben could hear her footsteps through the ceiling. *And soon I will hear 'Wakey wakey, Neigh-Neigh'...oh, she is soooo predictable,* giggled Ben, listening out for his mother's words. But instead of hearing chatter, he heard footsteps hurrying back downstairs again. "Sarah's not in her room. I'm just going to check the farm," his mum stated, her face a little red. Ben shrugged again. His sister was probably hiding somewhere, ready to jump out at him; she often did childish things like that.

An hour later, Ben was sitting on his bed reading his favourite book, 'A Hundred Facts About Cows'. Suddenly, his mother came running into his room. "Ben!" she puffed, breathlessly. "Ben, Sarah's gone!" Ben looked at her in alarm.

"Have you checked the stables?"

"Yes, of course I have!"

"The fields?"

"Everywhere Ben, I've checked everywhere! Your sister has gone!"

Ben couldn't believe it, his sister had to be *somewhere*. He took his iPad off the shelf. He clicked into Contacts and tapped on Sarah's picture. *Where are you? Mum is looking for you!* he typed, feeling his face getting redder and redder with rising panic. He pressed 'Send', but instantly heard a 'ding' from Sarah's bedroom. Wherever she was, she had left her iPad behind, so he could not contact her *at all.* This was ridiculous. There must be a way of finding her. After a long night of searching, Sarah had still not returned. The family soon realised this was not one of her childish games. She was really gone. They called the police, and all of Sarah's friends but nobody had seen her.

The next morning, instead of waking up excited, Ben was miserable; miserable because it was his tenth birthday, and Sarah was still not home. His mother came into his room, holding a chocolate cake with ten candles on it. The cake was decorated to look like a very messy cow; he didn't know if the icing had exploded, or his mum had intended for the cake to look like that. His mum was smiling at him, but sadness shone out of her eyes more than the sun shone through the window. "Happy Birthday, Moo! Make a wish," she said, with a happy tone, that was obviously fake. Ben sat up suddenly. This was it! If he wished for his sister to come back, it might come true! Birthday wishes always came true!

He closed his eyes and wished as hard as he could: *I wish my sister would come back! I wish my sister would come back! I wish my sister would come back!* He blew out the candles, looked at his cake and smiled at his mother. He felt a bit better now. "I'm ten, I'm ten! Mmmm, delicious! Chocolate?" he asked, grinning from ear to ear. "Yes, do you want to come downstairs? There are presents," his mother replied, obviously trying hard not to cry. "Good idea, mum! How many presents?" Ben answered, getting out of bed. "Four or five from me and your father, and one from Neigh-" she stopped, mid-sentence. She didn't want to upset Ben *or* herself, further. "It's alright mum," Ben said quickly. "So, one present from Sarah? At least she bothered this year!" he gave a soft chuckle.

Ben trudged down the stairs, his mother trailing

behind him. "I'm so excited! I wonder what everybody bought me!" he shouted, even though he knew perfectly well that his mother was only one step behind him. He needed to show her everything was going to be ok. Ben opened the living room door and began to tear open his gifts.

* * *

4. The Winged Beast Tells All

Sarah looked around her. *Where was she? Where had this winged beast taken her?* The creature let go of her, and Sarah stood up slowly. *What was it? Why had it taken her?* The creature growled, "STOP! Do you want me to hold you so you cannot move?!" Sarah froze. The monster could *speak.*

She stepped closer and examined the creature. It had a large, black body, with huge wings, and tall black horns on its head. There were smaller sharp horns on its wings. Glowing red eyes. Shining white teeth. *Razor-sharp teeth*, Sarah noticed. "What...what do you want with me?" Sarah stuttered. "I don't want anything *from* you," the creature laughed, "I just want you!" The laughter sounded evil, like a hyena's laugh. Sarah didn't like it. "What - what are you?" Sarah whispered, her eyes wide with fear. "I'm a dragon, can't you see?!" The dragon chuckled, a deep rumbling chuckle.

A dragon - it made sense. Horns, teeth, wings, an unfamiliar creature. But dragons didn't exist. "You're probably wondering why I'm here?" he asked. "My name is Onyx, in case you wanted to know," he added, giving a sly, toothy grin. Sarah stayed silent. "You're Neigh-Neigh, am I correct?" he asked, his eyes narrowing while he circled Sarah. "No, that's just my nickname. I'm Sarah," she whispered.

"Sarah," Onyx emphasised her name, as if checking to see if he liked the sound of it. "Would you like to learn about dragons, *Sarah?*" She slowly nodded. So, Onyx told her tales of dragons, so *many* dragons. He described each of them in so much detail, Sarah almost felt she could see them on a giant screen in her head. Surprisingly, only one dragon seemed scary; the dragon who destroyed all other species - the DragonReaper. She was so glad DragonReapers were now extinct!

"...and I'm a TwilightTwirler!" he ended, raising his head, proudly. "Now you're probably wondering why you're here?" Onyx asked, his eyes narrowing for the second time. Before Sarah could answer, Onyx continued, "There is still one of each species of dragon left on this planet, including me of course!" He grinned. "They all disguise themselves to help stay alive, especially the weaker species such as the MoodDrifter. They need a *companion.*

"For years I have watched you; your first steps, I have watched you growing up, your work in the stables. You are strong Neigh-Neigh." Sarah stared in disbelief. Onyx continued, "I have watched you for your whole life, and I have chosen you. We can train together, of course, we have a friendship that nothing and no-one can break. All you need to do, is sign," he ended, his grin looking even more shiny and *toothy* than before. *A friendship? I've only just met you!* thought Sarah, confused.

"Sign what, exactly? When will I see my family again?" Sarah replied, her arms crossed, and her eyebrow raised.

"You have to sign *this* to get the answers you require," Onyx responded, as a sheet of black paper appeared. A black pen was in Sarah's hand. Sarah hesitated, then removed the lid from the pen. Bringing the pen towards the paper, she wrote the words *Sarah Shell* on the dotted line. The ink glowed red like blood. Suddenly, Sarah's eyes turned red too. "Now, you asked if you could see your family again...the answer is yes. But you have a job to do first."

"I... I have one more qu..question," she stuttered, suddenly feeling absolutely terrified. "Ask me," Onyx replied, his fiery red eyes twinkling. "You said that the seven dragons are in disguise - what were you disguised as?"

"Isn't it obvious, Sarah? A simple horse cannot run

fifty-two miles per hour! But a dragon can...I am Snowball!"

Sarah gaped. Her beloved horse was not a horse after all. All these years, she had been riding a dragon.

5. The Missing Child

Ben looked out of the window the next day. It was snowing. He started to wonder if his sister was ever coming home. A big fat tear rolled down his cheek. It was horrible knowing that a member of your family was out in a storm somewhere, probably shivering, scared, alone. "Come home, Neigh-Neigh," he whispered. "Everybody is looking for you."

He suddenly froze, *what was that noise?* There it was again. It became louder, and Ben suddenly recognised the sound. Someone was screaming. A *girl* was screaming. Ben ran down the stairs; was it Sarah? He had to find out what was happening. He hurriedly pulled on his coat and ran out the front door. He heard the scream again, but this time it seemed to be coming from *above* him. He looked up in alarm. The girl's screams grew fainter and fainter. He searched the sky. Then he saw it; a huge wing of some unknown creature had just moved silently above a particularly large cloud. He rushed back inside, up to his bedroom. He looked through the window again and heard an almighty roar.

"Moo?" His mother touched his arm, making him jump.

"Oh, it's you," he replied.

"Was that you making that noise?" she asked.

"N... yes, sorry, I'll keep it down," he lied; he didn't want his mother to be even more scared than she already was. She had enough to worry about.

"Alright darling." She walked out of the room, closing the door quietly behind her. Ben was breathing heavily.

What *was* that he heard? What was that he *saw*? Was that really a girl he had heard screaming, or was it just his imagination? His eyes moved back to the window. Across the lane, he saw a man and a woman on the doorstep of the neighbouring farm. They were looking up at the skies too. What if they were the girl's parents? They looked frightened, confused. He heard a muffled cry. The father shouted, "Ginny, *Ginny!* Where are you?"

Later, Ben thought about what he had seen and heard. This had to be linked to Sarah's disappearance somehow. He walked slowly downstairs, his mind racing. Tapping his father on the shoulder, he asked, "Dad, can I go outside – I need to meet someone?" "Yes, don't wander too far though, and keep an eye out for Neigh-Neigh," he replied, absent-mindedly, wiping his left eye with a tissue. "Thanks!" Ben called, as he raced out of the door.

He ran across the lane towards the couple he had seen through his window. "Hello, I heard you calling. Has your daughter gone missing?" he asked the lady and gentleman, who looked around the same age as his own parents. "One minute she was here, the next she was gone!" the man whispered. "Sir, my sister has disappeared too, just like your daughter. There's no sign of her; it must be linked, somehow! Can I look in your garden for clues, please?" he asked, his eyes staring hopefully at the couple. "Your sister? Yes, I heard about that. Of course, anything to get our GinGins back," wept the woman. "The garden gate is open around the side of the house." Ben thanked them. He found the open gate. *What were those marks in the wood?* He realised the gate was covered in deep gashes, that looked awfully like claw marks. He walked into the garden cautiously.

It was a nice little area; a table and three chairs were placed in the middle of the snowy grass, which had been cut very neatly. A giant oak tree stood at the end of the garden. Ben searched the garden curiously. There was a little patch of tulips peeping through the snow-covered soil next to the oak, and further along, was a huge pond.

It was almost a lake; it was so large. Ben walked deeper into the wonderful garden. Suddenly, he stopped dead in his tracks, his heart beating dangerously fast. There were footprints leading from the pond in the direction of the house. The tracks obviously belonged to an animal, but big, very big. The footprints mysteriously stopped in the middle of the garden. They might belong to that flying creature he saw earlier! The beast could have jumped out of the pond, or down from the tree, and grabbed the unsuspecting Ginny.

He tip-toed back towards the pond and stared, shocked. There was an exceptionally large hole in the ice. He was right, the creature *had* jumped out of the lake. There were fish bones floating on the top, and one lonely carp hiding in the dark water. He left the garden, walking across the lane back home. There was a journalist interviewing the frightened couple.

He overheard part of the report: *'Shock as another child disappears: Sarah Shell aged ten, now joined by neighbour, Ginny Song, aged just seven years old'.*

6. Ben Finds Out

A week passed, during which time another child disappeared: an eleven-year boy called Jiang, originally from Asia, who was on holiday, visiting his cousins. Ben knew some things about the beasts that he believed had taken the children: There was more than one, but each of them had claws and teeth. He guessed that some sort of water creature had taken Ginny, and he believed a red, fiery monster had taken Jiang. There had been rumours of such a creature lurking near where Jiang had been staying but obviously nobody believed it.

There had been a huge hole in the ice-covered pond in Ginny's garden, but he had also caught a glimpse of a large, winged *thing* flying high in the sky when he heard screaming around the time of Ginny's disappearance. As for Sarah, he still had no clues, but they all had to be linked. The police were having no luck finding the missing children, and there had been no possible sightings for days, but Ben wouldn't give up. He would keep searching until Neigh-Neigh was back home annoying him like she always did.

Ben lay on his back in bed, staring at the ceiling. It was morning, and he only had a few minutes until his mother would come in to wake him up. Ben came to a decision: he was going to find out what was happening, and he was going to do it today. A moment later, his mother opened his bedroom door, as he predicted, and said, "Morning Moo, breakfast is ready." Ben leapt out of bed, somehow, he was going to find Sarah, and he would find her today!

Ten minutes later, after wolfing down his bacon roll, Ben jumped up from his seat, startling his parents, and rushed upstairs to get dressed. He chose his camouflaged shirt and trousers and put on green socks. He ran to the bathroom to brush his teeth; he was concerned his minty breath might make it harder for him to track the monsters in secret – *what if they picked up his scent?* - so he made sure he drank lots of water afterwards.

He rushed downstairs and grabbed his binoculars from the kitchen drawer. "I'm going to go...er...bug hunting!" he lied, spying his sister's butterfly net next to the binoculars, and picking that up too to make his story seem more convincing. He rushed out of the house before his parents could ask any questions, slamming the front door behind him. He breathed in the fresh morning air as he hurried off.

The woods were situated at the end of the fields belonging to his parents' farm. He was going there first. Ben entered through the trees and started to walk along the narrow path. Suddenly, he felt something brush past his legs. He looked down in alarm. "Oh, Dog, what are you doing here? You gave me a fright!" Ben beamed with relief. Dog looked up at him and barked as if to say *Ben, I want to find her too, don't you know that?* He rolled on his back happily as Ben gently stroked his head. "Stay next to me now, ok?" he whispered to the dog as he started to walk along the path again. Dog stayed very close to his side.

Twenty minutes later, the boy and his faithful four-legged friend reached the middle of the forest. It was creepy, silent. Ben tackled the thorns so he and Dog could fight their way through. When he reached another large thorny bush, Dog crawled underneath. Ben waited for him to leap out the other end, but he didn't. He waited a few more minutes, but there was still no sign of Dog.

"Dog! Here boy!" he called and whistled. All of a sudden, Dog jumped out of the bushes and landed at Ben's feet. "Dog! Where were you? I thought I'd lost you too!" He let out a sigh of relief and tickled the animal's ears. As Dog barked with delight, the ground began to tremble beneath Ben's feet. He stared at his companion; *what was happening?* Dog began to bark excitedly.

Without any warning, the animal began to shake. With an almighty howl, Dog began to grow right before Ben's disbelieving eyes! He grew and grew. His black and white fur turned hard and shiny, like a shell. He had *scales.* His already sharp teeth and claws grew longer and longer. With a popping sound, two *wings* sprouted out of Dog's back! Ben could not believe his eyes. *I must be dreaming,* he thought. Dog now resembled the creatures he believed had taken his sister and the other children.

Dog was a dragon.

7. The Mooddrifter Of The Forest

Dog the dragon was weirdly beautiful. He had rainbow scales and silver horns on his head. The scales formed a silver helmet, leading down his nose and around his eyes. Ben could not believe it. His cute, funny dog, was a dragon? All of a sudden, the dragon's scales turned yellow. "What is going on?!" Ben said aloud. Ben didn't feel scared, the dragon looked quite friendly and kind.

"I'll tell you whatever you want to know," said the dragon in a soft voice. "OMG you can talk!" Ben fell backwards in shock. "I could always talk Moo, but now you can understand me," said the dragon. "What have you done with Dog?!" Ben yelled. "I am Dog, Ben, can't you see?" the dragon said quietly. "I needed to disguise myself from humans, so I have been living as your pet for years." "Wh... what sort of dragon are you?" stuttered Ben. "I am a MoodDrifter. I spit venom and I can camouflage. I sleep in trees, hanging by my tail, and I change colour depending on how I feel. As you can see, I have turned yellow, which means I am excited! You finally get to see the real me!"

"Wh... why now?" asked Ben still trying to understand what was happening. "All the dragons have chosen their companions, and I have chosen *you,* Moo". "A companion? Other dragons? You won't eat me Dog, will you?" begged Ben. "No, no, I only eat plants and fish!" the dragon made a grumbling noise that sounded a bit like he was laughing. "The only carnivores are FlameFlyer and TwilightTwirler!" the dragon paused. "And DragonReapers, but they're extinct. They are the reason that there are barely any dragons left!"

This was so much for Ben to take in! It still didn't seem real, how could it? There was a yellow dragon standing where his dog used to be, and it could *talk*! "Oh, and please call me Sparkle. I never did like the name *Dog - it never* sounded pretty enough for a beautiful girl like me!" the dragon giggled again. "You're a *girl!* Oh, this is too much!" Ben huffed. He started trying to piece together all the information he had learned about the missing children, and the things this creature had told him.

There were other dragons. They were choosing companions, whatever that meant. Could this help him find Sarah? "Dog, I mean, Sparkle? Do you know who the other dragons have chosen as their companions?" he asked. Sparkle looked down at him, "I do...and you do too, Ben. HydraHunter chose Ginny Song. FlameFlyer chose Jiang, and TwilightTwirler chose," Sparkle hesitated. "TwilightTwirler chose your sister."

"I need you to be my companion Ben, all you have to do is sign this!" insisted Sparkle. A piece of golden paper suddenly materialised, and a rainbow pen magically appeared in Ben's hand. Ben considered this. "On one condition, I want to see my sister, I want to see Neigh-Neigh," Ben pushed. "You can, I promise! Please trust me Moo, I've never let you down before!" Sparkle pleaded. "OK, it's a deal," and he took the lid off the little pen.

Slowly, he wrote the words *Benjamin Shell* on the dotted line. His eyes shone emerald-green as he finished. "So, what do we do first?" Ben asked. He was getting excited. He had his own dragon – that was so much cooler than having cows or horses! "Do I get to miss school?" he asked hopefully. "No, no," Sparkle chuckled. "Education is the most powerful thing you could possess, even more powerful than a dragon!" she smiled a toothy smile. "The other children missed school," Ben grumbled, looking down at the soil, disappointed. "Not all dragons feel the same as me, Moo. But it's the holidays now so you don't need to worry about school for a while."

Sparkle paused. "Now, the first thing we need to do is get you to your sister."

* * *

8. The First Challenge For Sarah

Back on the island, while Sarah slept, Onyx the TwilightTwirler would pace up and down in his colossal cave. He knew the first challenge he needed to set Sarah involved her survival skills...if she had any. *How* he would test her was another matter. He set fire to a bush in frustration. It wasn't a big fire, so it soon fizzled out. This was going to be a long night.

The early morning sunshine shone in Sarah's eyes, waking her. Every morning, since arriving at the island, she had collected strong sticks, and pieces of wood she found on the beach, to make a shelter in the trees. A treehouse. She was about to start again this morning when she heard the dragon. "Neigh-Neigh! Come here!" Onyx bellowed. She hurried across the sand to the dark cave where she found Onyx waiting for her. "I have considered your first challenge as a companion," he said. "I would like you to find me some food - by yourself." *That shouldn't be too hard,* Sarah thought. She had been searching for coconuts and bananas to feed herself for days. "I eat meat, but as there are no animals on this island, I need fish," continued Onyx. "You have until sunset to find me enough fish to eat."

Sarah hurried off to the river. Ok, this wasn't going to be as easy as she first thought. She had tried fishing once, but it hadn't gone well. This time she didn't have a fishing rod either, she was going to have to use her hands!

It seemed impossible at first. The fish were slippery and wriggled out of her hands every time she got too close. Eventually, after what seemed like hours, she managed to get into a good rhythm. As with most things, practice makes perfect! Scoop, grab, throw! Scoop, grab, throw! The little pile of silvery fish on the riverbank was getting bigger, very slowly.

As the sun was slowly setting behind the trees, she carried her haul back towards the cave. *Now for the cooking,* she said to herself. She grabbed three long, thin branches from a tree, and some vines. She stabbed two of the long branches in some wet sand, then tied the third horizontally using the vines. She went to search for wood she could use for a fire. She formed some sticks into a pyramid. Rubbing two sticks together as her father had taught her on their last camping trip, they eventually began to smoke, and a small flame appeared. She laid the sticks down onto the thicker branches, and watched the fire get bigger and bigger. Using her earrings as hooks, she hung the fish on the sticks above the fire and watched them cook. *Next time, I'll use my earrings to catch the fish!* She smacked her head with the palm of her hand, as she realised her task could have been made so much easier, if she had only given it more thought.

When all the fish had cooked, she put out the fire with some sea water, and walked to the cave. "Here, Onyx. I cooked them all too," she said proudly. The dragon looked down at the pile of cooked fish. "Acceptable for a human who is new to this," he smiled kindly. "Although for future reference, I can cook them myself," he laughed and snorted a small burst of fire out of his nostrils. He began to eat.

When Onyx had finished his meal, he looked at Sarah, his red eyes twinkling. "Are you ready for challenge two?" he asked. "What is challenge two?" Sarah asked, worriedly. "Learn to ride me while I am flying!" Onyx flapped his wings.

Sarah stood up excitedly. "When do we start?"

* * *

9. The Tale Of King Sabusa

Sparkle, with Ben clinging on to her horns for dear life, landed softly in a clearing that was unfamiliar to Ben. "Where are we?" he asked. "We are on the dragon's island: Isla Sabusa," Sparkle replied, proudly. *Wow.* Ben knew he had kept his eyes closed for most of the flight, but how long had they been flying, for them to arrive on an island he'd never heard of?! Ben sat down on the rocky ground. "What does Sabusa mean?" he asked. "In the dragon language of Dracon, it means Leader and Creator." Sparkle announced, "I really need to teach you more about us - oh! I'll tell you the tale of King Sabusa!" she said, excitedly, sitting bolt-upright, and she started telling the magical story to Ben.

"It all started on this island, long, long ago..." Sparkle began. Ben closed his eyes. It was almost like there was a huge cinema screen in Ben's mind, showing him the story as it unfolded. He felt he had travelled back in time. The island looked a lot different back then; it was completely covered in a huge jungle. Sparkle described a green Flame-Flyer. "There was only ever one green FlameFlyer," he heard Sparkle say, as if from a distance. Suddenly, he saw King Sabusa, sat on his throne of leaves. "Approach," he boomed. A TwilightTwirler flew closer to the King. "Sire," he said, "The DragonReapers' want a meeting." While Sparkle told the story, Ben imagined he could see King Sabusa's eyes widen with shock. "THE DRAGONREAPERS?" he bellowed "NO! THEY ARE NEVER, EVER WELCOME HERE!" "Yes sire," the TwilightTwirler spoke hurriedly and flew away. King Sabusa paced up and down. "Eight eyes, four heads...the deadliest of us all." He looked worried for a moment, but this soon turned to fear as he heard an ear-splitting roar. "They're already here!" he cried in terror.

Six DragonReapers screeched as they surrounded his throne. "We heard you don't want us," the fearsome creatures whispered in haunting voices. "No, no, that's not true! I have always welcomed all dragons to Isla Sabusa!" the King said quickly. The DragonReapers inched closer. "No, we heard everything Sabusa," the six scary creatures said together, as if with one voice. King Sabusa shook his head worriedly, "N..no, I d..don't know what you heard, b..but that is not so," he stuttered, shaking with fear. Sabusa was cornered. There was no escape. "LIES! We know everything Sabusa!" The DragonReapers, suddenly showed their needle-sharp teeth and terrifying claws...

31

Ben realised Sparkle had stopped speaking, and the 'cinema screen' in his head had shut down. He opened his eyes, blinking. "I think that's all you need to know," said Sparkle. "But wait, what happened to King Sabusa?" he asked.

Sparkle turned away, whispering, "He was never seen again".

* * *

10. The New Dragon

L ater that day, Sparkle returned Ben to the woods near his farm, and transformed back into Dog. As he walked down the lane towards his house, he could see so much activity, and people everywhere! *What was going on?* Ben reached his house, and his parents were frantically talking over each other. "Moo! Where have you been?!" his mother asked, excitedly. "Sarah is home! Do you hear me? Your sister is home!" his father hugged him so tightly, he struggled to breathe. Ben saw Sarah over his father's shoulder. He pushed towards her and gave his sister a huge hug. "Dragons?" he whispered in her ear. "Dragons" she whispered back, nodding and smiling.

After the fuss had died down, and the reporters and police had left the family alone, Sarah and Ben rushed upstairs to talk. Sarah told Ben all about Onyx, the mysterious island and how she had learned to hunt. Onyx had decided that Sarah should see her family and friends now that her survival skills had improved, so he had dropped her back to the farm earlier that day. Ben then told her how he had been investigating her disappearance, which led to him discovering his own dog was a dragon called Sparkle!

"So, is 'Snowball' back in the stable then?" Ben giggled. "Noooo. Onyx said he had a meeting on Isla Sabusa." Sarah replied, twirling her blonde hair with her finger worriedly. After everything Ben had told her about the island's history, she was quite concerned for her dragon companion. "Hmmm...Sparkle never said anything about a meeting?" Ben wondered aloud.

Suddenly Dog came rushing through the door, whining at the two children, and tugging on Ben's jeans. He obviously wanted them to follow him. The siblings looked at each other, got up and followed the dog out of the house. They ran all the way into the woods. Suddenly the ground started to rumble in a way that was familiar to Ben. Dog howled and transformed back into Sparkle. "Moo, Neigh-Neigh, I need to show you something! Quickly, jump on my back!" The two children obeyed, and Sparkle flew up into the night sky.

Soon they landed on Isla Sabusa; for Ben it was the second time that day! He looked around. This time it was different. There were other dragons waiting for them. Seven dragons in total, if you counted Sparkle and Onyx. "There's another one!" realised

Sarah, pointing under a large rock pile. Indeed, there was. A glowing yellow baby dragon was sitting, looking up at them! A FlameFlyer and Onyx were surrounding it in leaves. "Our newest dragon," declared Sparkle, glowing with pride - literally, glowing bright orange! "This, my dear children, is Glow, our PyroTwister. She is the first of her kind. Laramie the LeafCrawler found her egg in the soil while digging for bugs. This draco must have survived somehow, when the DragonReaper killed all our ancestors, and has been undiscovered all this time. Without the warmth of another dragon's breath, she would never have hatched!"

"Did Laramie hatch her?" asked Ben. "No, Onyx did," replied Sparkle. "Onyx can produce just the right type of heat - not too hot - for an egg. TwilightTwirlers were always the ones to care for abandoned or lost eggs." Sarah was astonished. "Can we take a closer look at Glow?" Sarah asked Onyx. "Yes, come closer. Ash can tell you all about Glow's powers." Onyx replied, nodding towards the FlameFlyer.

Sarah slowly moved closer to the baby dragon, and softly stroked its head. "PyroTwisters can create huge fires and can control the heat of the sun," Ash explained in a deep voice. "They can also transform into human-form as well as animals, and other dragons; something we have never managed to do." Ash stopped as Glow sneezed, transforming into a ginger cat. "She needs to learn to control her powers" laughed Ash. Glow transformed into a much larger dragon before Sarah's eyes. She tried to blow fire, but a small wisp of smoke came from her nostrils. She turned back into her normal self.

"Can she talk?" asked Sarah, tickling Glow's belly. "Not yet," said Ash. Sarah looked thoughtful for a moment. "Say 'Hello!' Hel-lo! Go on Glow, say hello!" she said gently to the dragon. Glow ignored her. Sarah tried again. "Listen, hel-lo Glow! Say hel-lo!" Glow looked up at her. "Hewo!" Glow squeaked. "Hewo! Say hewo!" she repeated in an extremely sweet voice. The other dragons stared. Sarah and Ben giggled.

* * *

11. The Eight-Eyed Stare

The next day, was back to normality for Sarah and Ben – the holidays were over. They arrived at school quite early for a change, so they sat quietly in their seats waiting for their classmates. The room soon filled up with noisy children. Bella, who was sat next to Alice, started giggling slightly, and asked loudly, "What *is* that smell, Alice?! It smells of *farm animals*!" Alice pinched her nose, while Bella pretended to faint. They couldn't stop giggling at their 'joke'. Ben and Sarah tried to ignore the 'Duo of Disgust' as they had secretly named the two girls. At that moment, Mrs. Hound came in. "Good morning, class!" she said brightly. "Today we are starting a new topic! Would anyone like to guess what we will be learning about?" A few hands shot up, including Ben's and Sarah's.

"Alice?"

"Plant life, miss?"

"No, not plant life. Ben?"

"Farmyards, Mrs. Hound?"

Mrs. Hound smiled at the boy. "No, I'm afraid not Ben. James?"

"Eight eyes!"

Mrs. Hound looked confused. "Pardon, James?"

"Eight eyes! Eight eyes were staring at me through the window!"

Mrs. Hound sighed. She was used to silly answers from certain children. "Nonsense, probably just a spider. The topic is... Ruthless Romans."

There were a quite a few groans, followed by a couple of gasps of delight. *Can't please everyone!* thought Mrs. Hound. Ben started to think about what James had shouted out – *eight eyes.* In Sparkle's story of King Sabusa, he remembered that Dragon-Reapers had eight eyes...coincidence?

Later in the dinner hall, word had spread about the 'eight eyes'; it was the hot gossip of the day. Ben grabbed Sarah by the arm. "Get off!" she shouted. "Shhh! Sarah..." he whispered, then told her what he had been thinking about. "Don't be silly, Moo! DragonReapers are extinct!" Sarah said, laughing. Ben let go of her arm. "There could still be some left! There *are* other dragons, after all!" Sarah considered this; it did make sense! "You know what," she said, "you could be right." She hated admitting this. Her brother was *usually* wrong, but that wasn't what she hated; she hated the idea that Onyx, Sparkle and all the other dragons could be in danger. "We need to meet with the dragons. Tonight," she declared.

That evening, after their parents were safely tucked up in bed, Sarah woke Ben, by shaking him roughly. Ben rolled out of bed and stared at her, trying to remember what they were going to do. Sarah was already dressed. Ben had gone to bed fully dressed, to save time. "Let's get Dog and go to the woods," Sarah whispered, and they quietly left the house. Once Dog and the children were in the woods, their four-legged friend changed into her dragon form. They explained what had happened, and Sparkle agreed that if there was even the slightest possibility that James had seen a DragonReaper in school, the other dragons needed to be warned. They flew to Isla Sabusa as quickly as Sparkle's wings could carry them.

"Onyx! Where are you?" Sarah shouted, once they landed on Isla Sabusa. "Neigh-Neigh? Is that you?!" they heard their fiery friend bellow. "What are you doing here?! Actually, there's no time to talk - we have a big problem!" They followed Onyx to the cave where Glow now lived. "What's the matter?" asked Ben, confused. Laramie was terribly upset, whimpering and groaning as if in pain. "Glow has gone! Som... something st..stole G..Glow," she sniffed. The children looked at each other. Their fears may have just come true.

* * *

12. Trickster!

Ben and Sarah could not believe it. Poor Glow! They investigated all around the empty cave. Suddenly, they heard a violent scraping noise above them. "Get inside, quickly!" whispered Onyx. They hurried into the cave and listened carefully, as the scraping grew louder. The noise caused stones to fall from the roof of the cave. As suddenly as it started, the scraping stopped.

The children heard heavy footsteps stomping towards the cave opening. A grey, spiky, horned head came into view, then another, followed by a third. And fourth. Eight eyes stared into the shadows. "A DragonReaper!" gasped Sparkle. She turned a deep shade of purple, the colour of fear. Onyx, already partly hidden in the dark shadows, moved further back into the depths of the cave. Sarah and Ben tried covering themselves with leaves, but it was a useless hiding place.

The DragonReaper moved closer and sniffed with its huge nostrils; its fiery eyes darting across the cave. It spotted the children and opened its giant mouth..."Hewo! Say hewo!" the scary beast cried in a squeaky voice. Ben and Sarah looked at each other. *What?!* The DragonReaper began to shrink, smaller and smaller and then turned yellow - it was Glow! "Oh Glow! You little trickster!" laughed Sarah in relief. "Did you try to visit us in school you naughty draco?! So, you are the 'eight eyes' that James thought he saw!"

Sparkle and Onyx crept out of the shadows. Onyx was chuckling, and Sparkle had turned bright pink with embarrassment. "Oh Glow, you funny draco! We're going to have to keep a closer eye on you," Onyx said with a grin. Sarah stroked Glow. "Hewo! Say hewo!" Glow was starting to sound like a parrot! "Trickter! Glow trickter!" "It sounds like she's saying, "Go tricksters!" doesn't she?" laughed Sparkle, now back to a calmer light blue. "Yes!" giggled Sarah.

"Gosh, it's getting light now," said Ben, "We need to get home, before our parents wake up!" The children said their goodbyes and climbed onto Sparkle's back, tired but relieved that they had said goodbye to DragonReapers for the last time.

13. The Dragon Population
Grows Again

Two years passed by; Sarah was now thirteen years old, and Ben had recently turned twelve. They had continued to be dragon companions, and Sparkle and Onyx still set them challenges from time to time. They didn't hear much about Jiang anymore, but they saw Ginny walking home down the lane sometimes. They never discussed the 'D' word with her though.

The dragons no longer lived on Isla Sabusa - with its tragic history the dragons had decided it was time to move on. They had recently discovered a huge island deep inside an old volcano. Lava had not flowed from the volcano for millions of years. It was unbelievably beautiful, and private – perfect for mythical creatures who were not supposed to exist. Could this be their new home?

One sunny morning, Glow, who was now a fully-grown PyroTwister, (although her voice still had a slightly squeaky tone sometimes), glided towards the volcano. "Are you *sure* you saw it here, Suzu?"

she shouted across to her friend. It's not one of your tricks is it?" asked Onyx, who was also flying with the youngster, along with Ash the FlameFlyer, and Sparkle. "No, not a trick for once!" answered Suzu, the RogueRacer. He was well-known for generally annoying the other dragons as often as he could. "Over here!" Suzu yelled, leading the group as they flew after him. "Here," he halted, and settled down to the ground. "Dig here, Ash."

The FlameFlyer stepped forward to a large lump of grey sand. He began to dig with his razor-sharp claws. After a few moments he let out a gasp. Onyx stepped forward to look. Dragon eggs lay in a nest. "Those are new eggs!" he said, surprised. The others peered into the nest. "But that means that there must be another dragon!" gasped Sparkle. Onyx sniffed the sand. "No, there is a whole herd," he said quietly. Onyx softly blew fire just above the grey sand, careful to only allow the heat, and not the flames, to touch the sand. "Extinguish," he said to the fire and magically the fire obeyed. As the smoke started to disappear, the dragons gasped with delight; the sand had melted away, revealing several other nests holding dragon eggs. *How could this be?*

Suddenly, they heard swooping wings overhead. They ducked, just in time to see a herd of completely unfamiliar dragons landing on the nests! A FlameFlyer stepped forward. "I haven't seen you before," he said suspiciously, studying each of the dragon friends in turn. His eyes settled on Glow. "And I have certainly never seen you." Glow smiled nervously, "My name is Glow, and I am a PyroTwister. I am the only one of my kind as far as I know" she said. The FlameFlyer turned away. "Welcome to Isla Draco, home to the survivors of the DragonReapers," he said. Sparkle stepped forward. "There aren't any DragonReapers here, are there?" she asked, quite frightened at the thought. "No, you will be safe here. Feel free to come and go as you wish. Explore!" the dragon replied and flew up to a large rock holding a nest of golden eggs.

That evening, the dragons returned to their human companions. Onyx and Sparkle told Sarah and Ben all that they had discovered on the new island. "So, there are more dragons?" asked Sarah excitedly. "Yes!" Sparkle replied, "So our little herd are not the last of our kind!" Sarah and Ben exchanged worried glances at each other. *What if the dragons no longer needed human companions?*

"You won't leave us, will you?" asked Ben, in a small voice. Onyx and Sparkle looked at the children sadly. "One day, but not just yet," the larger of the two creatures said in a deep voice. "But why?" asked Sarah, tearfully. Onyx looked down at the young girl. "We chose human companions we could trust to keep us alive," he said. "We thought we were the last of our species.... but now we know we were wrong. It would be unfair of us to keep taking you from your family, from your home." Sparkle looked at Ben, who hadn't said a word.

"You knew this was going to happen, Moo, I mean, Ash said goodbye to Jiang more than a year ago". The children sniffed. They understood, but that didn't mean they had to like it.

"Now, would you like to have another flying lesson?" Onyx asked the children.

They smiled and nodded.

14. The Gift

It was incredibly early on Sarah's fourteenth birthday. She waited in bed excitedly, her mind whirring with thoughts of what everyone had bought her. Clothes? Technology? Something horse-related? There were so many things she would be happy with.

The next hour passed so slowly, but Sarah soon heard the footsteps of her family coming towards the bedroom door. The door burst open, and her dad, mum and Moo came into view - with a very tasty-looking cake!

"Happy birthday to you,

happy birthday to you,

happy birthday to Neigh-Neigh,

happy birthday to you!" they sang.

Sarah jumped out of bed. "Thanks guys! Ooh carrot cake! My favourite! Wow mum, you did a decent job of icing that horse!" Sarah beamed. Her mum smiled, shyly. Her baking always tasted delicious but didn't always look as good as it did in her head.

"You have gifts downstairs!" said Ben, almost as excited as Sarah was. "Come on! You're going to love my present!" Sarah and Ben raced down the stairs, their mother and father walking sensibly behind them. Sarah beamed as she looked around the room. Ten perfectly wrapped presents were sitting by the fireplace.

"Cake or presents first?" asked her mother. "Presents please!" Sarah replied, although she wished she could have both at the same time. She knelt beside the pile of presents and looked at the tag of a small one. She read, *To Neigh-Neigh, Happy 14ᵗʰ Birthday, Love Mum and Dad.* Sarah smiled at her parents as she opened the present. A green t-shirt with white horses on it - perfect. "Thank you!" she beamed.

Sarah opened all the other presents from her mum and dad; a new equestrian helmet, a shiny saddle, and a new book about horses were soon followed by a couple of family board games, the latest book by an author she really enjoyed, some new trainers and a new case for her iPad. Then she opened Ben's present. "Oh, it's perfect!" She exclaimed to Ben as she added the little silver dragon to her charm bracelet. "Thanks Ben!" Mum and dad looked at each other confused. *Dragon?* Ben smiled. "I'm sure some of your friends have presents for you too." said mum. "Ben said they would meet you in the forest. Weird!"

When the siblings arrived at the forest, they saw Sparkle and Onyx waiting for them. "Happy birthday Neigh Neigh!" they said to Sarah. They had presents for both children instead of just the birthday girl. The gifts were exceedingly small but turned out to be very precious indeed. Sarah and Ben removed the delicate paper. Sarah gasped. Inside was an incredibly beautiful necklace. Attached to it was a sparkly dragon egg that seemed to glow. Ben's dragon egg was attached to a keyring. The children were speechless.

"The eggs are magic," Sparkle announced. "They represent the magic that is inside each of you." "We give them to you now so they will help you remember us when we leave." said Onyx, his deep voice unusually gentle. Sarah looked sad and confused. "How?" "The eggs will protect you from any danger that crosses your path. When you turn twenty-one, the eggs will hatch into dragons, who will return to Isla Draco to be with us."

* * *

15. They Say Goodbye

A week passed since their meeting with the dragons. Sarah wore the necklace every day, and Ben kept the keyring with him always. When Ben and Sarah had returned to the house with the gifts, on Sarah's birthday, their parents were curious to know how one of their friends had the money to get something so valuable, and *where* they had found such unusual gifts. *Who knew their kids were so interested in dragons these days?* Sarah simply explained that one of her friends, Joanna, had a relative who made jewellery, and had been kind enough to make something for Ben too.

Mr. and Mrs. Shell were not totally convinced; they had never heard either child speak of a friend called Joanna, but they let the subject go. They had been worried about their children for quite some time; they were secretive, often disappearing for hours at a time. And even though they were grateful Sarah had returned to them unharmed all those years ago, they never really had found the underlying cause of how, or why, she had disappeared in the first place. The unusual, expensive-looking gifts were the icing on the cake – they needed to know what was going on with Moo and Neigh-Neigh; next time they left the house on one of their 'walks', the parents would follow them.

It was the weekend. Just a regular Saturday. Ben and Sarah had just left to go to the forest, as they did every weekend, but this time they wouldn't be alone. Five minutes after the children left, Mrs. Shell had pulled on her boots and winter jacket, and Mr. Shell had done the same. Leaving the house, they could see the children up ahead. They waited for them to enter the forest before following. The forest had always felt creepy to Mrs. Shell, so even when walking with Dog she avoided the area as much as possible. "What's that?" asked Mr. Shell suddenly. "It's just an owl, don't be such a baby." replied his wife, sounding braver than she felt. They stumbled over stones and sticks until they suddenly saw their children up ahead. Mrs. Shell pulled her husband into a bush, out of sight.

Ben and Sarah seemed to be talking to the trees. Now they were laughing! Mrs. Shell stared into the shadows. She was sure she had just seen a glimpse of red. *Was that fire?* What they saw next was just too unbelievable. They watched as their beloved pet, Dog, howled. They heard a deep rumbling sound, as the ground began to shake. Dog was no longer the faithful pet they trusted to look after their sheep.

Dog was big, *really big*. He had *wings*. He could *speak*! Mrs. Shell let out a whimper. Her husband covered her mouth with his hand. "Sshh! They'll hear us!"

They listened carefully to the voices of their children. There was another deeper voice coming from the shadows where Mrs. Shell had seen the red light. And of course, there was a voice coming out of the creature formerly known as Dog. The children were no longer laughing. "No!" Mr. And Mrs. Shell heard their daughter cry. "No, please, stay another year!" The children seemed to be pleading with the shadows, and then their shoulders dropped as if they had accepted whatever was going to happen.

Suddenly, they saw what seemed to be a flock of huge birds flying out of the trees into the sky. These creatures were too big to be birds. *The size on those wings!* The startled parents saw their precious Moo and Neigh-Neigh staring up at the sky, waving, tears rolling down their cheeks. Afterwards, they saw their children holding the egg-shaped charms on their new gifts. They seemed to *glow.* They left the woods quietly, and rushed home.

❋ ❋ ❋

Since that crazy Saturday in the woods, Sarah and Ben no longer disappeared for hours on end. They

51

still visited the woods but always came back looking miserable. There were no new expensive-looking gifts, no whispering at the dinner table. Whoever – no, *whatever* - they had been meeting all this time seemed to have gone for good. Their parents felt sorry for the brother and sister in a way, they seemed so sad.

Actually, there was one other strange thing that happened. A little crystal ornament appeared in the Shell's garden, hanging from the apple tree. It was shaped like a bird, a little song thrush. Nobody admitted to buying it or putting it in the tree; it just *appeared.* Even through the changing seasons, the strongest winds, the deepest snow drifts, that crystal song thrush continued to hang from the apple tree, glittering in the sun, and glowing in the moonlight.

* * *

Epilogue

Onyx, Sparkle, Ash and Laramie left Ben and Sarah in the woods, and headed back to their forever-home, Isla Draco. The growing herd of dragons continued to stay safe and happy, away from the distant threat of Dragon-Reapers. However, one little dragon no longer lived on the island hidden in the volcano. A certain PyroTwister had decided she had another place she would much rather be...

Glow stayed behind at the farm. She was a master of disguise as all the dragons and the children had learnt over the years. However, now she had chosen a disguise she would stick with forever. A little crystal song thrush so that she could watch over her beloved Moo and Neigh-Neigh as they grew up. She saw the children achieve many remarkable things.

Sarah eventually became a teacher, got married and had children of her own. Ben had followed in his father's footsteps and had taken over the family farm, where Glow continued to hang in the apple tree. He was also married and had one daughter. As the years went by, Glow watched Ben and Sarah become grandparents too. She stayed with them until it was their turn to say goodbye.

So, if you hear the melody of a song thrush coming from your garden, maybe, just maybe it's the sign of a new adventure just around the corner.

The dragons are waiting to meet you.

AFTERWORD

Dear Reader,

Thank you for buying my book! I hope you enjoyed reading it. With this being my first book, I know, deep down, that it can be improved upon, so I am already considering writing a second edition, expanding on the characters and some of the story-lines.

Best wishes,

I. R. Davies

ABOUT THE AUTHOR

I. R. Davies

Hi I hope you like my book - it is my very first one. But to be fair, I am only ten, so please be kind!

I came up with the idea for this book from my fascination with mythical creatures.

I live in Wales, with my mum and cat, Clover, who is an absolute furry wrecking ball! I also have a chihuahua named Millie who is very affectionate.

Always believe in magic - my mum says you're never too old!

PRAISE FOR AUTHOR

My baby girl has always dreamed of becoming an author, so I am incredibly proud that she has managed to write her first book at such a young age! In my opinion, it is fabulous; every chapter ends on a cliffhanger which certainly made me want to read more. I can't wait to see what ideas she comes up with next!

I hope you enjoy her first book as much as she enjoyed writing it.

- T. L. DAVIES

Printed in Great Britain
by Amazon